# FURRY AND FLO

STONE ARCH BOOKS
A CAPSTONE IMPRINT

J SERIES FURRY and FLO

Furry and Flo is published by
Stone Arch Books
A Capstone Imprint
1710 Roe Crest Drive
North Mankato, MN 56003
www.capstonepub.com

Text and Illustrations © 2014 Stone Arch Books

Library of Congress Cataloging-in-Publication Data
Troupe, Thomas Kingsley.
The big hairy secret / by Thomas Kingsley Troupe ; illustrated by Stephen Gilpin.

    p. cm. -- (Furry and Flo)

Summary: Fourth grader Flo Gardner and her mother have just moved into the Corman Towers apartment building, and she is pretty sure she does not like it--the boy werewolf next door is all right, but the monster spiders have got to go.

  ISBN 978-1-4342-3858-0 (library binding) -- ISBN 978-1-4342-6423-7 (ebook) -- ISBN 978-1-62370-033-1 (paper over board)

1. Werewolves--Juvenile fiction. 2. Spiders--Juvenile fiction. 3. Monsters--Juvenile fiction. 4. Friendship--Juvenile fiction. [1. Werewolves--Fiction. 2. Spiders--Fiction. 3. Monsters--Fiction. 4. Friendship--Fiction.] I. Gilpin, Stephen., ill. II. Title.

PZ7.T7538Big 2013

813.6--dc23

                                    2013002776

Artistic effects: Shutterstock/Kataleks Studio (background)

Book design by Hilary Wacholz

Printed in China by Nordica.
0413/CA21300443
032013      007226NORDF13

# THE BIG HAIRY SECRET

## BOOK 1

BY THOMAS KINGSLEY TROUPE
ILLUSTRATED BY STEPHEN GILPIN

# TABLE OF

# CONTENTS

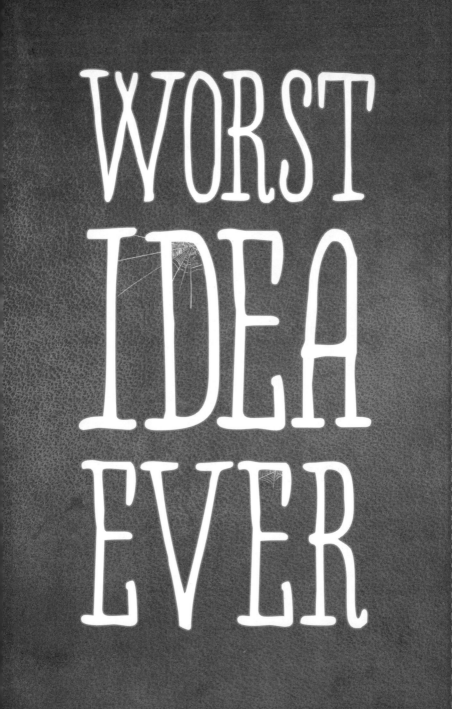

# CHAPTER 1

"Are you excited to start fourth grade at your new school, Florence?" the school secretary asked. She smiled kindly from her seat behind the registration desk. A nameplate sitting on top of the desk read "Mrs. Franklin."

"That's not my name," the girl said, glaring at the woman. She clamped her lips closed into a frown and crossed her arms in front of her chest to show she meant business. "And, no, I'm not."

"Flo, don't be rude," her mom scolded. She reached out and put a hand on the girl's shoulder.

"Oh, I'm sorry. Is your name Flo or Florence?" Mrs. Franklin asked. She furrowed her eyebrows as she studied the forms spread in front of her. "I have 'Florence M. Gardner' written here."

"No, that's right," Flo's mom replied. "Her real name is Florence, but no one calls her that. She's hated that name since she was two. Everyone calls her Flo now."

"That's because Flo is my real name," Flo grumbled. She looked around the school office. It wasn't as nice as her third grade school had been, or even the one she'd gone to for second grade. Then again, nothing could top the first grade and kindergarten school. It seemed like the schools got a little uglier and a little smellier with each move.

"Well, I think Florence is beautiful," Mrs. Franklin said. "The name, I mean. Not that your daughter isn't. That is, she's a delightful child. What I meant to say is . . . oh, dear."

Mom just kept right on smiling. "I know what you meant," she said. "And thank you. We're so grateful you're letting us get Flo registered. Between starting a new job and moving into a new place, it's been a hectic few days."

"Oh? When did you move in?" Ms. Franklin wrote something on the form, stamped the bottom of the piece of paper, and slipped it into an envelope.

"This afternoon," Mom said, nodding toward the window. "Right after we finish up here, actually."

The Gardners' over-stuffed minivan was visible through the half-open blinds. Mattresses were tied to the roof with rope. Chair legs, lamps, and anything else they could squeeze in poked out of the open windows.

Ms. Franklin smiled. "Well, at least you were able to find your lunchbox," she said, nodding toward the metal box balanced on Flo's lap. "But you won't need that until school starts."

"You never know when you'll need a lunchbox," Flo said quietly. She put her hand protectively over the cartoon Dyno-Katz on the lid. "Besides, my dad gave it to me."

"Well, isn't that nice?" Ms. Franklin remarked, clearing her throat nervously.

An uncomfortable silence followed.

"We're excited for a new change, aren't we, Flo?" Mom said finally. She put her best smile on to show just how excited she was.

"About as excited as I was for the last new change," Flo said, not sounding excited at all. Not even a little bit.

"Well, everything is all set here," Ms. Franklin said. "See you in the fall, Flor —"

Flo shot the lady a dirty look.

"I mean, Flo," Ms. Franklin said quickly. She fixed her glasses and smiled. "We look forward to seeing you in a few months."

"Okay," Flo said. She slid off the chair and made sure to bring her lunchbox with her. "Let's get out of here, Mom."

As her mom drove their van through the city, Flo was amazed by how big everything seemed. The city was much bigger than the last city they'd lived in a few years ago. There were people everywhere, crossing the street, hurrying in and out of buildings, and pushing past each other on the crowded sidewalks.

*You'd think the city would seem smaller, since I'm bigger*, Flo thought, shifting her leg. Her foot was stuck between a toaster and a magazine rack crammed together on the floor. She pulled her foot free, yanking it right out of the sneaker.

As the minivan turned a corner, a book tumbled out of one of the poorly closed boxes. It slid across the top of the front seat and bonked Flo on the back of her head. She

picked it up and fired it into the back with all
of their other stuff. She rubbed her sore head
and sighed loudly.

"Things are going to
be different this
time, Flo," Mom
said, tapping
the top of the
steering wheel.
She leaned forward
in her seat and peered up
at the tall buildings. Just then, a glob of white
splattered the windshield.

"Pigeon poop," Flo said.

"Don't talk like that," Mom said.

"Even if it's true?" Flo asked, pointing at
the glass.

Mom flipped on the windshield wipers,

smearing the mess on the glass and making it even worse.

"Yep. It'll be different this time," Mom said with a laugh.

Flo couldn't help but laugh a little, too. After a moment, she sighed and peered out the side window. The tall buildings blocked out the sun. Flo thought it felt like the city was swallowing them up.

# FERDINAND

# CHAPTER 2

The Corman Towers apartment building
was pretty much smack dab in the middle
of the city and a lot taller than Flo had
expected. Their new home wasn't much of a
home at all, in her opinion. It was more like a
thousand different people's home — she just
happened to have a room in it.

Flo and her mom lugged their first few
boxes through the lobby and up to an elevator.

The passenger cars squeaked and whined as they moved up and down.

"Are we on the top floor?" Flo asked.

"No," Mom said. "Floor seventeen."

When the elevator car arrived, Flo stepped inside and looked at the panel of buttons. There were 34 floors. Some of the lighted numbers were burned out. A couple had been smashed in. Flo pushed the cracked button for the seventeenth floor.

"We're kind of right in the middle," Flo said as the doors slid closed. The light inside dimmed and then brightened again. The elevator jerked, hitched, then groaned before it began to rise.

"We'll get used to this," Mom said, pushing her loose hair out of her face. "I promise. It's kind of an interesting place, though, isn't it?"

Flo read some of the graffiti scratched into the metal wall of the elevator and raised her eyebrows. "Yeah," she muttered. "It's interesting, all right."

* * *

The elevator jerked to a stop at the seventeenth floor, and the doors slowly groaned open. Flo took a step out and something zipped right past her. It startled her enough that she fell back and landed on her rear end. The box of silverware she was carrying clattered to the floor.

"Holy socks!" Flo cried as Mom helped her up. "What was that?"

She brushed off her shorts and peered down the hallway. A boy dressed in just a pair of white underwear paused in a doorway down the hall. He stared at her for a few moments before disappearing back inside. The door to his apartment slammed closed behind him.

"Okay," Flo said. "There's some crazy kid roaming the halls in his underwear. What kind of place is this, Mom?"

"Don't be silly," Mom said. "It's no big deal. He was probably just embarrassed and ran to hide."

"Uh, okay," Flo said.

Flo and her mom made about a hundred trips back and forth, carrying the rest of their stuff up to the seventeenth floor. Flo couldn't help but notice that their new home was right across the hall from where Underwear Kid had disappeared. Not exactly a comforting thought.

When Mom went back downstairs to park

the car, Flo stood in the doorway and looked into their new apartment.

"Maybe if I don't go in, we can move somewhere else," Flo whispered under her breath. Suddenly, she heard a creaking sound nearby.

"Hi," a voice said from behind her.

Flo turned around and saw a boy with thick, jet black hair peering at her through the partially opened doorway across the hall. Even though he was mostly hidden, Flo could see that he was still only wearing underwear.

*So much for him being embarrassed*, she thought.

"Um, don't you believe in wearing pants?" Flo asked.

The boy shrugged. "It's summer," he said. "Who wears pants?"

"Normal people. And you should too," Flo said, turning her head. "It's weird talking to someone who isn't wearing pants."

"Okay," the boy said with a shrug. He closed the door, and Flo heard a soft *Thud! Thud! Thud!* as his feet padded across the floor inside his apartment.

A few moments later, he opened the door again. This time he wore a pair of plaid shorts and nothing else. "Better?" he asked.

Flo shrugged. *Where the heck is Mom when I need her?* she thought. She knew it would be rude to just head into their apartment and close the door on her new neighbor . . . even though that's exactly what she felt like doing.

"I'm Ferdinand," the boy said. "But everyone calls me Furry. You know, for short."

"Furry?" Flo repeated. "That's kind of a funny name."

"I'm kind of a funny kid, I guess," Furry said. He shrugged like it was no big deal. "What's yours?"

"I'm Flo," Flo said.

"Flo," Furry said. He shook his head. "Are you serious?"

Flo gave the boy the best dirty look she could manage. "Your name is Furry, and you're asking me if I'm serious?" she asked in disbelief.

"You're kind of crabby sometimes, aren't you?" Furry asked. "I get crabby too when I can't go outside."

"I am not," Flo snapped.

The sound of the elevator grinding to a stop at the seventeenth floor cut Flo short.

She turned to see her mom emerge, dragging the last of their boxes.

"Well, it was nice to meet you," Furry said. "Let me know when you're not so crabby. Maybe we can hang out or something."

Before Flo could say another word, Furry closed the door and disappeared. End of conversation.

"Who were you talking to?" Mom asked as she walked up. "Was that Underwear Kid?"

"Furry," Flo replied, smiling a little. "He said his name is Furry."

"Furry?" Mom repeated. "Huh. Well, okay then." She stepped past Flo and into the apartment. "Is he nice?"

Flo shrugged as she followed Mom inside and closed the door behind them. "He's weird," she said finally. "Just plain weird."

"Well, it's good to make friends," Mom said. "Even weird ones, I guess."

Flo looked around at the apartment. The place was really old looking. Dingy-looking carpet covered the floors. A rust-colored light fixture hung from a chain in the corner

of the living room. The glass in one of the windows was cracked, and there was a light brown stain on the ceiling. Flo wasn't sure she wanted to know what it was.

"Home sweet home," Mom said. "It's okay, right?"

Flo nodded even though she knew without a doubt that her dad would've hated the place. Dad had always been trying to get them into a nicer house whenever he could. Just thinking about him made Flo clutch her lunchbox even tighter.

Flo knew her mom was trying her best. She'd never had to work back when Dad had been alive. But now that he was gone, everything was different. Mom didn't have much experience, which meant she had to take whatever job she could find. More often than not, that meant they ended up moving somewhere new.

Flo tried not to complain every time they had to find somewhere cheaper to live. But their new apartment at Corman Towers was so different from the nice house their dad had bought all those years ago. It didn't seem fair that their whole life had to change.

"You're thinking about Dad again, aren't you?" Mom said. She reached out and drew Flo into a hug, clutching her tightly.

Flo buried her face in her mom's chest and did her best not to cry. "A little," she admitted finally. "I just miss him sometimes. All the time, really."

"I know," Mom whispered. "Me too." She softly kissed the top of her head. "But he's always with us, you know."

Flo nodded again. But no matter what her mom said, it wasn't the same. Her dad was gone, and he wasn't ever coming back.

# CHAPTER 3

It was way past dinnertime by the time Flo's mom took a break from unpacking. That was always the first thing Mom did whenever they moved to a new place. Flo usually waited to unpack — she was never sure how long they'd be staying.

While Mom finished putting stuff away, Flo headed into the kitchen and opened the mustard-yellow refrigerator. The bright white light was the only thing inside and it nearly blinded her.

"What are we having for dinner?" she called into the other room.

"Oh, right," Mom replied. "We need some groceries, don't we?"

"Yeah," Flo said, closing the door. "That might help." She headed into the living room, expecting to see Mom busy putting things away. "Should we go to the store?" she asked as her stomach growled loudly.

Her mom swiped at something Flo couldn't see. She flicked her hand as if something was caught on it, and then wiped her hands on her jeans.

"What are you doing?" Flo asked.

"It's kind of webby in here," Mom said.

"What do you mean, 'webby'?" Flo asked.

"You know, spider webs," Mom said looking around. "They're everywhere. I hope the building doesn't have some sort of spider problem."

Flo took a deep breath as Mom grabbed her car keys and led them out the door. *Good thing I didn't unpack anything yet*, she thought. *We won't be here long, either.*

* * *

Since the refrigerator and cupboards were completely bare, Flo and her mom bought one of practically everything at the grocery store. They came back loaded down with bags. Together they hauled them to the elevator, rode to the seventeenth floor, and lugged them to the apartment. Flo set her bags down as her mom fumbled for the door key. Then, one by one, they brought them inside.

There were a lot of bags.

"Is that all of them?" Mom asked. She started to pull open cupboards and put stuff away.

"I think there's one more bag," Flo said. "I'll get it."

When Flo returned to the hallway for the last sack of groceries, she noticed something was wrong. There was a giant bite mark on the side of the bag! Inside, she saw a half-eaten head of lettuce and a shredded cereal box (with the free magic-ink pen missing). Worst of all, the box of Popsicles she'd picked out was gone.

"No way!" Flo cried. She squatted down and examined the evidence like a real detective. There were no clues nearby. But when she stood up and headed farther down

the hall, she found a Popsicle stick with large bite marks in it. The end was splintered and stained orange.

"Must have been a dog or something," Flo muttered. She opened her lunchbox and put the splintered stick inside.

As she headed back down the hall to her own apartment, Flo remembered something. Corman Towers didn't allow pets. She'd seen the big sign at the rental office when she and her mom had picked up their keys.

*If pets aren't allowed, how did our groceries get so messed up?* Flo wondered. She wasn't going to let this go. Her Popsicles were gone, and she wanted justice.

Without thinking twice, Flo walked across the hall and knocked on Furry's door. He seemed like a nosy kid, which meant he'd probably know if someone on their floor had a giant dog.

After a moment, she heard footsteps.

"Hello?" a woman's voice called from the other side. "Who is it?"

Flo smiled sweetly. "It's Flo Gardner," she said. "I'm your new neighbor across the hall."

The door opened and an older woman peered into the hallway. She had curly gray hair and looked old enough to be Flo's grandma.

"It's nice to meet you," the woman said. "I am Mona Babbitt."

"You must be Furry's mom," Flo said. "I met him earlier, and I need to ask him something."

"Ferdinand is doing laundry in the basement," Mrs. Babbitt said. "He'll be back in an hour or so."

"Do you know if someone on this floor has a big dog or something?" Flo asked. "Our groceries were —"

"Oh, no," Mrs. Babbitt interrupted. "Not here. No pets anywhere here."

Before Flo could ask anything else, her own apartment door opened.
She turned and saw her mom studying the mess from the shredded grocery bag in front of their door. When she turned back

around, Mrs. Babbitt was gone.

"Jeez, Flo," Mom said. "I know you're hungry, but couldn't you have at least waited until we got everything inside first?"

"It wasn't me!" Flo said, folding her arms. "Seriously, Mom, we've got a problem. Some kind of wild animal must've gotten into our groceries while we were unloading them."

"Oh, that's crazy," Mom said.

"It took all of the Popsicles!" Flo said, pointing to the shredded brown bag. "They were right here! This thing means business."

But no matter what Flo said, Mom pretended it wasn't a big deal. And Flo knew why. Unless a flaming meteor from outer space was about to drop onto Corman Towers, Mom would act like their new place was just perfect.

Even though it wasn't.

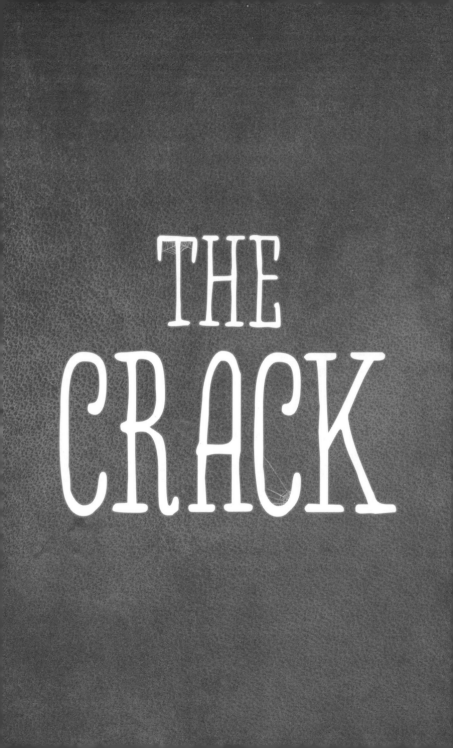

# CHAPTER 4

If there was one thing Flo was really good at, it was making sandwiches. And she wasn't just good for a ten-year-old.

No. Flo was better than most grown-ups at the fine art of sandwich making. So, once the remaining groceries were put away, she got to work making turkey sandwiches for her and Mom. She decided to make a spare one, just in case, and stuck it in her lunchbox for later.

Then Flo and her mom ate dinner in the living room, surrounded by the mountains of boxes.

"I should call the cable company," Mom said halfway through her sandwich.

"What's the rush?" Flo muttered. Secretly, she hoped they'd move within the week. The way things looked, it was a definite possibility.

Mom kept chattering about the things she needed to do: get a new driver's license, forward the mail, call the insurance company. Flo didn't listen. She couldn't stop thinking about the grocery problem. It was driving her nuts. More than anything, she wanted a nice cold Popsicle after she finished her sandwich.

"I'm going to explore the building a little, okay?" Flo said as she finished the last bite of her sandwich.

"Okay," Mom said. "Just be careful and stay

inside. There are all kinds of weirdos out in the city."

"Great," Flo said, picking up her lunchbox. "I'm so glad we moved here."

"You know what I mean," Mom said. "But listen, we're going to make this apartment work, okay?"

"Well, if we don't, that's fine too, Mom," Flo said, putting her plate in the sink. "We just have to find the right place."

As Mom nodded quietly, Flo felt bad for what she'd said. She knew Mom was trying.

"I'll be back in a little while," Flo said.

"Okay, sweetie," Mom said with a smile. "Thanks for the sandwich. And be careful."

"I will," Flo said and pulled the door closed behind her.

* * *

It took Flo exactly three seconds to figure out where she was headed. Mrs. Babbitt had said that Furry was in the basement laundry room, so that seemed like a good enough place to start. Maybe he knew something about the grocery-mauling menace.

As Flo walked to the elevator, she heard it groan and grind as it headed down. Rather than wasting time waiting, Flo found a door covered in chipped paint that led to the stairs. She shoved it open with a squeak and heard it echo through the stairwell.

Flo looked down over the railing to the bottom of the stairs. Some of the landings were lit with a single bulb, while others were completely dark. She hurried down the stairs two at a time, scurrying past the darkened landings. When she reached the fourth floor, she saw something white on the floor in the corner of the landing.

"What *is* that?" Flo whispered, taking a cautious step forward. When she bent down, she noticed several more spread around on the ground. They looked like balled-up socks or giant cotton balls.

Flo stood up and backed away. "This place is filthy," she muttered, wrinkling her nose in disgust and continuing down the stairs. As she did, small wisps of spider web touched her face. Flo quickly swiped them away. The webs seemed to grow thicker as she neared the basement.

Flo opened the door with

a shove and entered a long hallway. She could hear the steady whir of a dryer at the end of the hall.

*That must be the laundry room*, Flo thought.

Flo continued down the hallway and poked her head into the laundry room. The machines looked old, and she was surprised they still worked. The *click-clack* of zippers and buttons on the metal dryer drum made a strange beat. She spotted Furry sitting on top of a large washing machine across the room, drumming his fingers on the metal lid.

"Hey," Flo said.

At the sound of her voice, Furry jumped about a foot in the air. He fell off of the washing machine and onto the hard floor with a loud *crash!* He quickly picked himself up and rubbed his shoulder.

"Ow!" Furry said. "You knocked my socks off!"

"You weren't wearing any socks," Flo said as she stepped into the laundry room. "But I'm glad your shorts are still on."

"Very funny," Furry said with a grin.

"So," Flo said, getting down to business. "Is there some kind of big dog or something living in the building?"

"No," Furry said quickly. "Why?"

"Something took a bite out of our groceries," Flo said, pacing the room. "Something big and hungry, from the looks of it."

"Huh," Furry said, looking away from her gaze. "That's weird."

"Whatever it was ate all of my Popsicles," Flo said. She sat down next to Furry setting her lunchbox next to her.

"Oh, that's not cool," Furry said. "Not during summer."

"I'm going to catch whoever did it," Flo said.

"I'm sure you will," Furry replied, watching Flo carefully.

The two of them sat for a few minutes, listening to the slosh of the washing machine and the hum of the dryer. Then Furry spoke up. "Want to see something awesome?" he asked.

Flo didn't want to seem too interested, but she did like things that were awesome. "Okay," she said with a shrug. "I guess."

Furry led Flo over to a cramped space behind the dryers. Rusty pipes ran overhead and lint balls covered the floor. Near the wall, a thin, blue line made a jagged slash across the floor. It almost seemed to be glowing.

"What is that?" Flo asked. She couldn't pretend to be disinterested anymore. The blue line was pretty cool.

"It's a crack in the floor," Furry said.

"I see that. Why is it glowing?" Flo asked.

"How should I know?" Furry replied. He crouched down and leaned in close. The light shining from the crack bathed his face in an eerie blue light.

And just like that, Flo forgot all about the Popsicles.

# CHAPTER 5

Furry and Flo sat in the laundry room for what felt like hours, staring at the crack. It was much bigger than Flo had first thought, at least a couple inches thick and nearly four feet long. The blue light shining through it was so bright that Flo couldn't see what was down there.

"What's down there?" Flo asked. She squatted down and set her lunchbox near her feet. She reached out to touch the crack, but Furry swatted her hand away.

"Don't touch it," he warned. "It's dangerous. I mean, it's *probably* dangerous."

Normally Flo didn't like some kid telling her what to do, but she let it slide. She was too mesmerized by the crack in the laundry room floor to say anything.

After a moment, the buzz of a dryer interrupted their study.

"Have you seen enough yet?" Furry asked. He stood up and started taking laundry out of the dryer.

Flo squinted at the blue crack for another second and then followed after her new friend.

*Just when I thought this place was weird enough*, she thought. *It gets weirder.*

"There must be a blue neon light or something in there," Flo said. "That's the only thing that makes sense."

Furry pulled a bunch of socks and T-shirts out of the dryer and dumped them into a plastic laundry basket without bothering to fold them. He stuck his head into the dryer to make sure it was empty, then slammed the door closed.

"Who'd put a neon light down there?" he asked. "That doesn't make any sense. Besides, it's not always glowing."

"Maybe someone turns it on and off," Flo suggested. But she knew that didn't make any sense either.

"Whoa!" Furry exclaimed suddenly. "Watch your feet." He leapt up onto the washing machine with a single, easy jump.

Flo's mouth dropped open, and she stared at Furry in surprise. She'd never see anyone jump so high or so fast.

Looking down, Flo saw a herd of giant spiders skittering across the floor. They seemed to be coming from the spot behind the dryers . . . where the crack was. Flo stepped aside. She'd never been afraid of spiders, but it sure seemed like Furry was.

"Oh, are you scared of spiders?" Flo teased him.

"Of course I'm not scared of them," Furry said. "I just don't like 'em. At all."

Furry's eyes never left the creepy crawlies as they scurried across the room. The spiders seemed to know exactly where they were going, and they headed straight toward the door. Now Flo knew why there were spider webs all over the building. Corman Towers had a serious spider infestation.

*One more reason to move*, Flo thought.

Once the spiders had disappeared, Furry relaxed a bit. Even so, he never took his eyes off the door.

"So how long have you lived here?" Flo asked.

"Since I was five or so, I guess," Furry said, hopping down off the washing machine. His bare feet hit the dirty, tiled floor with a loud slap. "I'm not really sure."

"Has this place always been this weird?" Flo asked.

Furry gave her a funny look. "What do you mean by weird?" he asked.

"Never mind," Flo said. She blew a stray strand of hair out of her eyes. Maybe Furry was so used to living someplace weird that it didn't even seem weird to him anymore. Maybe someday she would get used to living there.

*That's a scary thought*, Flo thought with a shudder. As she turned her head, she noticed more white, fuzzy things tucked away in the shadows. "What are those?" she asked, pointing across the room.

Furry hunched down low and looked where Flo was pointing. "Those?" he said. His face looked a shade paler. "Those look like spider eggs."

"What?" Flo cried. Her eyes grew huge. "Are you serious? Those things are enormous! There's no way they —"

She stopped as something long and black tore through the white covering. One spider leg was quickly joined by seven others. In seconds, a spider the size of a guinea pig tore out of the giant egg and stood on its spindly legs. It made a *clack-clack* sound as it crawled a few steps across the tile floor, heading straight for them.

"Okay, I'm done with laundry," Furry said. Before Flo could move, the boy ran out of the laundry room like his tail was on fire.

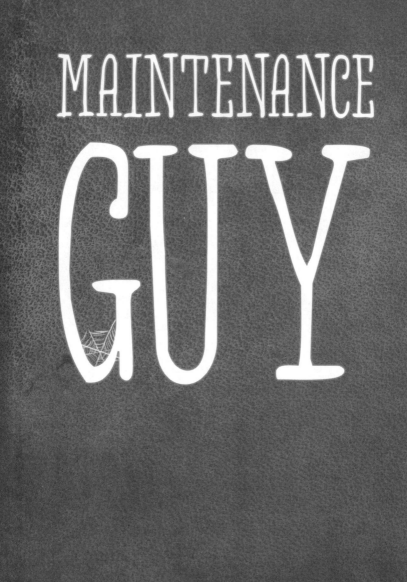

# MAINTENANCE GUY

# CHAPTER 6

"Furry!" Flo shouted. She felt silly shouting that ridiculous nickname out loud, but she didn't think shouting "Ferdinand!" would've been much better. She flew out of the laundry room doorway and saw Furry sprinting down the hall.

"Hey, wait up!" Flo cried, chasing after him. Her lunchbox banged hard against her leg as she ran down the dimly lit hallway. More spider webs clung to the ceilings and dark corners.

*This place is disgusting, even for a basement,* Flo thought. *Why are there so many spider webs everywhere?*

Flo was so busy looking around that she didn't notice Furry had stopped in the middle of the hallway. She slammed right into him, knocking him over and falling flat on her stomach. Her lunchbox flew out of her hand and clattered to the floor.

"What are you doing?" Flo shouted, picking herself up. She hurried over and picked up her lunchbox, clutching it protectively to her chest. Her T-shirt was covered in dust and grime. Flo brushed it off as best as she could, but it was no use. She was filthy.

"What am I doing?" Furry yelled. "You ran

into me!" He did a quick back flip to stand up, landing easily on his feet.

Flo stared at him in surprise. "Jeez, what are you, some kind of ninja or something?" she asked.

"No," Furry said with a quick, nervous smile and a laugh. "Don't be ridiculous. I'm not anything."

Just then, a door at the end of the hallway creaked open. An old man wearing a ratty, faded green bathrobe and the thickest pair of glasses Flo had ever seen stood in the doorway. Wispy white hair stood up crazily all over his head. His mouth was puckered into a frown, and he held a silver tray in his hands. It looked like a TV dinner and it smelled burnt.

"Um, hi," Flo said.

The old guy ignored Flo and turned to

Furry instead. "Ferdinand? Is that you?" the man asked, pushing his glasses up his nose. His tiny eyes squinted at them from behind the frames.

"Hi, Mr. Rockwell," Furry said. "Sorry about the noise. We just saw some spiders, and Flo here got scared."

"Hey, I wasn't scared," Flo protested. "You were the one who —"

"Whatever," Furry interrupted. "Mr. Rockwell is the maintenance guy for Corman Towers."

"*Was* the maintenance guy," the man corrected. "I'm retired. And please, call me Curtis."

*That explains a lot*, Flo thought. *No wonder everything in this place is such a mess. The janitor retired.*

"Oh, right, I forgot," Furry said. "Did they ever hire someone else to take your place?"

Curtis laughed like he'd just heard the funniest joke ever. He bent over, nearly spilling his charred TV dinner onto the dirty floor. When he stood up again, he clutched his stomach.

"Oh, that hurts," Curtis groaned. "Replace me? No way. No one else would ever want the job!"

Just then, Curtis seemed to notice the lunchbox Flo was still holding protectively against her body. "What do you have there, young lady?" he asked.

"It's my lunchbox," Flo said, clutching it to her a bit tighter.

"Whatever is in there sure smells better than my dinner," Curtis said, taking a step closer. As he did, Flo flipped the latch just to be safe.

"Do you know about the spiders?" Flo asked, trying to change the subject. "I think they're coming from the laundry room. There's a weird blue crack in the floor."

"Stay away from that blue crack," Curtis warned. Behind his thick glasses, his eyes grew wide. "Just pretend it isn't there."

"We should go," Furry suggested. He glanced nervously down the hall, as if he expected more spiders to appear at any second. "C'mon, Flo."

But Flo wasn't going anywhere without some answers. "What do you know about the crack?" she asked, nodding toward the laundry room.

"I know I don't want anything to do with

it," Curtis said firmly. He nodded at Flo's lunchbox again. "What do you have in there, anyway?"

Flo smiled. She popped the latch on her lunchbox and pulled out the turkey sandwich inside. "It's a turkey sandwich," she said. "Probably the best sandwich I've ever made. My dad always said to be prepared for anything. So, I always make sure I've got an extra sandwich. You know, just in case."

Curtis's eyes lit up, and his stomach growled loudly. "Smart man," he said quickly.

"I might be willing to share it with you," Flo offered. "But you have to tell us about the crack." She slammed the lunchbox shut.

Curtis peeked out into the hallway and looked both directions. When he didn't see anyone else, he nodded. "Deal," he said. "But be warned: I am not responsible. Now hand over that sandwich."

Flo opened her lunchbox and tossed Curtis the turkey sandwich. He quickly pitched his burnt TV dinner in a nearby trashcan and snatched the sandwich out of the air. Pulling it out of the plastic sandwich bag, Curtis immediately dug in.

"It all starts with this building," Curtis said around a mouthful of turkey and bread. "It was built a long time ago on top of an ancient seal."

"Like a seal you see at the zoo?" Flo asked, frowning. "The kind that barks and eats fish?"

"No, no," Curtis said, shaking his head. "A seal like a plug. It was built to seal off a doorway into another world."

"Another world? That's funny, Curtis,"

Furry said. He let out a fake-sounding laugh. "C'mon, Flo. We should go. It's getting late."

"In a minute, jeez," Flo muttered. She wanted to listen to the entire story. "Go on, mister."

"The seal was strong enough to keep the creatures from that world out of ours," Curtis continued. "It held for centuries, but in the past five years or so, something changed."

"What?" Flo asked, her eyes growing wide. She glanced over at Furry, who was busy fidgeting and biting his thumb. Maybe he was still too concerned about the spiders to listen to Curtis's story. Or else he'd heard it before.

"It cracked," Curtis said. "And now, anything can come spilling through that blue crack you found. And stuff does. Terrible stuff. I've seen it all."

"Like giant spiders," Flo whispered. "But what else?"

Curtis shook his head. "You don't want to know," he said. "Besides, I've said enough already."

Curtis crumpled up the now-empty sandwich bag and tossed it into a nearby trashcan. "It was nice to meet you, Flo," he said. And with that, Curtis closed the door in their faces.

# CHAPTER 7

"I told you we shouldn't have bothered talking to Curtis," Furry said once they reached the seventeenth floor. They stepped out of the rickety elevator and headed toward their apartments. "Now you lost a sandwich."

"It's fine. I make them all the time," Flo said. "Besides, aren't you curious about that crack?"

Furry shrugged. "Not really," he said. "I just thought it was cool."

"Not so cool if it's spitting out spiders and who knows what else," Flo replied.

When they got to their doors, Furry suddenly groaned.

"What's the matter?" Flo asked.

"The laundry," he said. "I left all of it downstairs."

Flo smirked. "Well, just be careful. You don't want creepy stuff crawling over your bare toes," she said. "Like spiders!"

"Very funny," Furry grumbled. "I guess I'll talk to you later."

"Yeah, okay," Flo said. "See ya."

Flo headed into her apartment and went straight to her new room. Even though it wasn't even dark yet, she was ready for bed. It had been an exhausting day. She brushed her teeth, changed into her pajamas, and threw a couple of blankets on top of her bed. Then she poked her head into her mom's room to say goodnight. Mom was lying face down on her bed, sound asleep.

"Night, Mom," Flo whispered, turning off the light.

Back in her room, Flo flopped down on the bed. The window was open a crack, and she could hear the sounds of the city outside — cars honked, bus brakes hissed, and someone shouted.

Flo stared up at the ceiling. She tossed and turned and tried to get comfortable, but it was no use. Finally she gave up and went to the window to pull open the blinds. She was surprised how bright it still was outside, hours after the sun had set. The city seemed to brighten the dusk.

"Cool," Flo whispered. She would have loved to go out onto the fire escape just outside her window, but it was too dangerous. Besides, their apartment was seventeen floors up.

As she closed the blinds, Flo heard a creak in the hallway. Knowing she wasn't going to fall asleep anytime soon, she dashed to the front door of her apartment. She pressed her eye against the peephole and gasped.

Furry stood in the doorway directly across the hall from Flo's apartment. He tried to slowly close his own front door. But it wasn't his sneaking out that surprised Flo. It was the box under his arm.

The box was bright yellow and had grape, cherry, and orange Popsicles on the front. "Popsicles," she whispered. Flo knew it wasn't a coincidence. Furry had stolen her Popsicles!

Flo wanted to burst into the hallway and confront him, but she stopped herself. She was too curious about what Furry was doing. She watched as he pulled the door shut behind him and dashed down the hallway toward the elevators.

Flo pressed her ear against the door and heard the sound of a door squeaking closed. *He must be taking the stairs*, she thought.

Flo grabbed her lunchbox and softly pushed open her own door, careful to keep quiet, and poked her head out into the hallway. It was empty. She slipped into the hallway and ran along the faded carpet. She needed to find out what Furry was up to and why he had stolen her Popsicles.

When she opened the door to the stairwell, she heard Furry's bare feet pounding against the cement steps above her. Curious, she followed him, trying her best to ignore the disgusting webs and spider eggs tucked into every corner.

After several flights of stairs, Flo was tired and out of breath. But Furry was climbing higher and higher. After a moment, she heard the squeal of a door opening above.

Flo hurried up the last few flights of stairs,

her legs burning. She stepped on a spider egg and cringed as it popped. When she reached the top of the stairs, she paused. Stenciled in red letters were the words:

Taking a deep breath, Flo opened the door and stepped out onto the loose gravel that covered the rooftop of Corman Towers. Furry was standing near the edge of the roof, staring off into the city. Clouds shifted past, moving quickly along the sky until the bright, full moon was exposed.

"Hey," Flo called. But before she could say another word, something amazing happened.

Furry changed.

One moment he was standing there in his underwear. Weird? Yes. But at least he was still a normal boy. In the next moment, dark gray fur exploded all over Furry's body. His feet and hands changed into paws. He threw his arms back and raised his nose to the sky. As he did, his face changed, too. His nose and mouth stretched out. His ears grew into points, and fur quickly covered them.

Flo's mouth dropped open and she stumbled, almost falling through the doorway. Before she could scream or run, Furry took a deep breath and howled at the moon.

Flo gulped. There were still a lot of unsolved mysteries at Corman Towers, but one thing had just become very clear.

Furry was a werewolf.

# CHAPTER 8

"You have got to be kidding me," Flo finally gasped.

The hairy little werewolf turned, still standing up on his very dog-like back legs and sniffed the air. His eyes got wide, and he bared his teeth.

"Uh-oh," Furry said.

Flo stood there, frozen, unable to run or scream.

"You can't tell anyone," Furry said. "Please."

"What do you mean I can't tell anyone?" Flo exclaimed. She pointed at Furry in horror. "You're a werewolf! Does anyone else know? How did this happen?!"

Flo couldn't stop staring.

"It's not my fault," Furry cried. He took a small, nervous step toward her. It seemed odd to see such a fearsome creature look nervous, but sometimes Flo had that effect on people. "I was born like this," he added.

Flo took a deep breath and tried to calm down. It was almost working until she saw the open box of Popsicles half hidden behind Furry. Instantly, her anger rose again.

"Those are my Popsicles!" Flo shouted, pointing again. "You're the one who stole my Popsicles and ate our groceries."

Furry lowered his head and looked ashamed. "I know," he said, letting out a whimper like a scared puppy. "It's just that I get really hungry when I change."

Flo took a cautious step closer, holding out her hand.

"What're you doing?" Furry asked and backed up a step.

"Trying to figure out if I'm dreaming," Flo said. "That's the only thing that makes sense. If I can touch your fur and it feels like fur, I'll know this is real."

Furry stopped and held out a paw. It was still small, like his human hand had been, but the fingers were longer. Sharp black claws had replaced his fingernails. Flo put her hand on top of Furry's. In that instant, she knew.

"This isn't a dream," Flo said in a whisper.

"Oh, wow. This is the craziest place I've ever lived. Ever."

"I've lived in some weird places before, too," Furry said quietly. "But I like it here. That's why you can't say anything."

Furry and Flo stared at each other for a minute. Neither of them said anything. Then Furry twitched a little and snatched up the box of Popsicles. With one swift movement, he unwrapped one and started to eat. Before Flo knew it, he'd eaten two more.

"Hey!" Flo snapped. For a brief moment she considered snatching the frozen treats away from Furry, but she didn't want to lose her fingers in the process. "Aren't werewolves supposed to eat, like, meat and people and stuff?"

Furry stopped inhaling Popsicles for a

minute and glanced up. Three different colored Popsicles hung from his mouth. "I don't know," he said. He swallowed the Popsicles whole and spit out the splintered sticks. "Maybe when I'm older."

Flo watched as Furry tore through the rest of the Popsicles in the box. This was unreal. She was kind of friends with a real-life werewolf. A werewolf who didn't want to eat her or anyone else.

Yet.

"Guess I'm not getting a Popsicle today," Flo muttered under her breath. She wasn't sure if Furry could hear her, but a moment later, an orange Popsicle, still in its wrapper, landed at her feet.

"I have awesome hearing," Furry explained. "You wouldn't believe the stuff I can sense when I'm like this. I can smell everything, see for miles, and hear people whispering six blocks away."

"That's handy," Flo said. She unwrapped her Popsicle and sat down on the roof. She'd almost forgotten she was wearing her pajamas. For a second she wondered if she should be embarrassed, but Furry didn't seem to care if Flo saw him in his underwear. Then again, he was covered in fur.

*A werewolf in a pair of tightie whities*, Flo thought staring at him. *You don't see THAT every day.*

Furry must have noticed her staring at him. "What?" he demanded impatiently.

"It's just . . ." Flo started to say. "What's with the underwear? Could you at least put on some shorts or something?"

"I get too hot," Furry explained. "You try having fur."

"Oh," Flo said. "I guess that makes sense." She took a bite of her Popsicle. It was kind of melted, but still delicious. "So, can you hear anything interesting now?"

Furry looked up from the mess of empty wrappers and sticks in front of him and froze. A rainbow of Popsicle colors dripped down his hairy chin. He let out a soft whine and looked up at the moon glowing above the city.

"What is it?" Flo asked. She stood up, suddenly worried.

"Something's coming," Furry barked frantically and spun around on all four paws. For the first time, Flo noticed the tail poking out through the waistband of his underwear.

"Where's it coming from?" Flo asked. "Should we run?" She was ready to hightail it down the stairs as fast as her legs would carry her.

Furry put his nose to the ground and moved closer to the edge of the building. Flo wanted to follow, but she didn't want to get quite that close to the edge unless she absolutely had to. She wasn't afraid of much, but heights weren't at the top of her "favorite things" list. Instead, she put her hand on the doorjamb and watched.

There was a loud scratching noise, and Flo felt her heart thump heavily in her chest. She gulped and watched the edge of the rooftop carefully.

*If Mom finds out I was up on the roof, I'll be grounded for a year*, Flo thought. *At least. Maybe we should get out of . . .*

"Run!" Furry suddenly shouted at the top of his lungs. He bounded toward her and the stairwell door.

Flo looked over to see what had made him so scared. Scurrying over the edge of the building behind Furry was the hugest, hairiest, most gigantic spider Flo had ever seen in her life. It was almost ten feet tall with long, spindly black legs. There were red marks on its stomach and what looked like a million eyes on top of its head.

As Flo watched, two giant-sized spider eggs dropped from the spider. It nudged them into a safe spot beneath a heating vent and covered the eggs with a silvery blast of webbing.

"Oh, great," Flo said. "I think that's the mom!"

"Get back inside!" Furry growled, racing for the door to the stairs. Flo hesitated for a moment, and the little werewolf barreled into her. The Popsicle flew out of her hand, and she landed inside the stairwell with a *thud!* Her lunchbox clattered to the ground beside her. Flo opened her mouth to scream, but ended up with a mouthful of werewolf hair instead.

"Gross," Flo grunted. "You're shedding! Get off of me!"

"Close the door!" Furry whined. He was up on all fours, running in circles like a dog who needed to go to the bathroom. "Hurry!"

Apparently Furry was terrified of spiders,

even as a werewolf. Flo jumped up with a grunt, making sure to grab her lunchbox off the floor, and went to the door. Through the opening, she saw the gigantic spider headed straight toward them.

Flo put her hand on the door and started to push it closed. Just then, the mama spider shot an incredibly long leg through the narrow opening between the door and the frame.

Flo ducked, barely avoiding a deadly blow. The spider's leg left a giant dent in the metal door. "Go, go, go!" she shouted.

Apparently Mama was coming in, and nothing was going to stop her.

# CHAPTER 9

Flo pounded down the stairs after Furry, her lunchbox banging against her leg as she ran as fast as she could. Her foot squashed another spider egg on the way down. One flight above, the giant spider emitted an ear-splitting scream.

"Sorry!" Flo shouted. She hadn't meant to squash the spider babies, but it wasn't her fault the mother had put them right on the stairs.

Flo heard the giant spider's legs clattering on the cement steps as it chased them down the stairs. Up ahead of her, Furry whined, darting down the steps three at a time.

*Werewolves, spiders, mysterious cracks in the floor*, she thought. *Now I'm running for my life. Nice place, Mom.*

"What're we going to do?" Flo shouted down to Furry. The little werewolf was speedy and had run almost two flights ahead of her. Werewolves were supposed to be fearsome, but Furry sure didn't fit the bill.

"Keep running!" Furry yelled frantically. "I don't want to find out what happens if she catches us!"

Flo stopped at the next landing. She could hear the spider thundering down the steps, getting closer and closer. It was moving way faster than Flo could. In no time at all it would catch up with her.

Flo gulped. She didn't want to be caught, but she also didn't want to lead the giant beast down into the hallways where people lived.

"Get up here, Furry!" Flo shouted. She didn't know if Furry would actually listen or not, but it was worth a try. As she waited, a chunk of ceiling broke free and crashed on the ground next to her. Another bit of concrete from the steps fell, landing on a giant spider egg nearby. The mother spider shrieked yet again.

*The eggs*, Flo realized. *She's trying to protect her babies!*

Just then, Furry poked his head around the corner of the closest flight of stairs.

"Why'd you stop running?" he asked frantically. His hairy, wolf face looked terrified. "That spider is still coming after us, you know."

Flo looked up and saw dust sifting down from the steps above her. They didn't have much time.

"Pick up as many eggs as you can," Flo said, motioning to the floor around them.

There were around eight or nine eggs just on the landing. Flo could see more tucked underneath radiators, nestled into the thick water pipes, and wedged into corners.

"What?" Furry asked. He looked up and whimpered. "But isn't that just going to make her angrier?!"

"Trust me," Flo said. "Just be careful not to crush them!"

Furry whimpered again. "I really want to go home," he said.

"Hurry up or you're not going to have a home!" Flo shouted. "That spider is going to tear this place apart!"

That seemed to jolt Furry into action. He started gathering up a couple of spider eggs. Flo tucked her lunchbox beneath one arm and started picking up eggs too. She pulled one from near the water main and heard the giant spider shriek again. It was true — the spider sensed when her babies were in danger.

*I really hope this works*, Flo thought. *Otherwise our stay here is going to be even shorter than I thought.*

# CHAPTER 10

Furry raced back and forth across the landing, sniffing frantically. His wolf nose perked up before he dashed up to the next landing. He returned with four more eggs. Flo counted nine in his arms. She had five.

The stairwell rumbled above them and legs poked between the flights of stairs. The shrieking spider was closing in, and she knew her eggs were being messed with.

"Good enough," Flo whispered. "We better get down to the basement, quick!"

Furry looked at Flo like she was crazy. "Why?" he asked. "We're just going to get trapped down there!"

Flo ran and Furry followed close at her heels. "I stepped on an egg when I followed you," she said. "I think that's why she's coming after us. She knows when the eggs are hurt or in trouble."

Furry stared at her in horror. "So then why are we taking them?" he asked. "We want her to chase us?"

"That's exactly what we want!" Flo said with a grin.

* * *

The eggs were slippery and squishy in Flo's hands, but she was careful not to drop them as she and Furry raced down the remaining stairs to the basement.

By the time they finally reached the basement level, she was pooped. Flo used her shoulder to nudge the stairwell door open. She raced through it with Furry hot on her heels.

"If a spider hatches in my hands, I'm going to scream," Furry warned her.

"Dude, you're a werewolf," Flo said. "Toughen up."

Flo paused in the hallway for a moment to catch her breath. Furry didn't seem out of breath at all. Instead, he paced anxiously back and forth across the corridor.

"Are we just going to leave these here?"

Furry asked, holding up the spider eggs. "Curtis isn't going to like that."

Flo ignored him. "We need to prop this door open," she said, motioning to the door leading to the stairs.

Furry stared at her with his wild yellow eyes. "Are you crazy?" he hollered. "If the door's open, that thing will be able to get down here!"

"It's already been down here!" Flo cried. "Duh! How do you think the eggs got inside?"

Flo looked around to find something to prop open the door. But for such a messy building, the hallway was surprisingly clear. Thinking quickly, Flo used her lunchbox to prop the door open. She hated to leave it in harm's way, but she didn't see any other option.

*Thank goodness I never leave home without my lunchbox*, Flo thought.

"You know it'll eat you first, right?" Furry said, keeping his eyes on the stairwell door. "You'll taste better than I will. I'm covered in fur."

"Yeah, yeah," Flo muttered and scooped up her eggs again. "Just wait for it to get close."

They didn't have to wait long. In seconds, the mother spider's legs poked through the basement door. Flo took off like a shot, sprinting down the hallway.

"Where are we going?" Furry asked.

"To the laundry room!" Flo shouted, darting inside. She just hoped no one else was washing their clothes. Luckily, no one was.

The spider's shrieks echoed through the hallway as eight giant legs skittered across the tile floor after them. Flo squeezed behind the dryers, making sure to keep the eggs safe. Looking down, she noticed that the crack in the floor was glowing even brighter than it had been earlier. It seemed to have grown wider, too.

"Great plan, Flo," Furry said, squeezing in behind her. "Now we're really trapped! Worst idea ever!"

"No way," Flo said. She watched the giant spider squeeze into the laundry room. She wasn't entirely sure this was going to work, but she didn't have another plan. A shiver raced through her as the first spider leg stepped over the bank of dryers.

"Throw the eggs into the crack," Flo cried. "All of them! Now!"

Furry didn't need to be told twice. He fired

the white eggs down into the blue crevice as fast as he could. Each egg made a loud *whoosh!* sound as it passed through the blue crack.

Flo started tossing hers down, too. The spider saw them and climbed over even more quickly. As the giant creature drew closer, Flo tossed the last one in and backed up against the filthy laundry room wall. Furry pressed close to her, covering his eyes with a hairy paw.

"I'm really sorry about your babies," Flo said. "We're not trying to hurt them. But you need to get out of here!"

The spider drew closer, then squirmed through the blue crack in the floor. A giant *whoooosh!* sound followed, and then the mother spider was gone.

Flo let out the breath she didn't realize she'd been holding.

"I . . ." Furry said, panting loudly. "I really hate spiders."

# CHAPTER 11

"I think that's the last of them," Flo said, tossing the final spider egg into the crack. She and Furry had spent the past two hours searching the whole building for more eggs. Furry's super sense of smell had come in really handy, and they'd collected several laundry baskets full of giant eggs.

"We should seal this thing up," Flo said after they'd finished dumping the rest of the eggs through the mysterious crack. "That way the spiders can't come back."

"Curtis told me it can't be closed up," Furry said. "Not forever, anyway."

Flo crossed her arms and stared at the blue light. There had to be some way to seal it, at least temporarily. Looking around the room, she spotted an old bedspread crammed in a corner. "This might work," she said.

Flo carefully stuffed the blanket into the crack. In moments, it was gone, replaced with a dingy, fabric-colored line on the floor.

"It's late," Flo said. She rubbed her eyes and let out a big yawn. "I need to get to bed."

"Yeah," Furry said. "I will too once I change back. But right now I'm starving."

"Okay," Flo said. "Well, I guess I'll see you around, then."

As she turned to go, Furry held out a paw to stop her. "Hey, wait a second," the werewolf said. "Sorry about your Popsicles. I can't always control myself when I'm like this."

Flo shrugged. "It's okay," she said. "Turning into a werewolf would probably make me pretty hungry, too."

"And please don't say anything about any of this," Furry added in a whisper. "Not to anybody. Not even your mom. I'd be in big trouble if people found out."

Flo nodded. "I won't," she said. "I promise. Your secret is safe with me, Ferdinand."

"Thanks, Flo," he said. "Hey, I meant to ask you, what's Flo short for, anyway?"

Flo took a deep breath and tried not get angry. After all, Furry didn't know better than to ask.

"Florence," Flo admitted. "That's my real name. I don't like it much at all. It was my grandma's name, but in all honesty I'm not sure she liked it either."

"Huh," Furry said. He nodded like he was thinking about it. "Yeah. I like Flo better, too."

"Thanks," Flo said, smiling at her new friend. "Well I'd better get back upstairs before my mom notices I'm gone."

"Me too," Furry said. "See ya around, Flo."

As Flo headed back upstairs to her new home, she got to thinking. Sure Corman Towers were dumpy and kind of creepy, but they were growing on her. And having a werewolf as a friend certainly didn't hurt.

*At least I won't be bored*, Flo thought. Who knows? *Maybe things are going to be all right after all.*

# THE AUTHOR

Thomas Kingsley Troupe writes, makes movies, and works as a firefighter/EMT. He's written many books for kids, including *Legend of the Vampire* and *Mountain Bike Hero*, and has two boys of his own. He likes zombies, bacon, orange Popsicles, and reading stories to his kids. Thomas currently lives in Woodbury, Minnesota, with his super cool family.

# THE ILLUSTRATOR

Stephen Gilpin is the illustrator of several dozen children's books and is currently working on a project he hopes will give him the ability to walk through walls — although he acknowledges there is still a lot of work to be done on this project. He currently lives in Hiawatha, Kansas, with his genius wife, Angie, and their kids.

# GLOSSARY

**anxiously** (ANGK-shuhss-lee) — worried

**dingy** (DIN-jee) — dull and dirty looking

**embarrassed** (em-BA-ruhsst) — feeling awkward or uncomfortable

**emerge** (i-MURJ) — to come out into the open

**evidence** (EV-uh-duhnss) — information and facts that help prove something or make you believe that something is true

**graffiti** (gruh-FEE-tee) — pictures drawn or words written on the walls of buildings, on subway cars, or on other surfaces

**opinion** (uh-PIN-yuhn) — someone's ideas and beliefs about something

# QUESTIONS FROM FLO

1.  My Dyno-Katz lunchbox is really important to me. My dad gave it to me, and it's all I have left of him. Plus, it's saved my butt in more than one situation. Do you have anything really important to you? Talk about what it is and why it's so special.

2.  I think Furry knows more than he's letting on about that crack in the laundry room. And like any good detective, I'm going to get to the bottom of it. Maybe you can help me out. How do you think the crack got there? Talk about your ideas.

3.  My mom and I move around — a lot. Have you ever moved? Talk about how you felt about it.

# PROMPTS FROM FURRY

1. I like Flo, but even so, I was worried about sharing my secret with her. After all, it's a pretty big one. Have you ever had a secret? Write about what you would do if you were in my shoes — or paws, as the case may be.

2. There are a lot of cool things about being a werewolf. (Constantly ruining my pants is NOT one of them.) Imagine that you could change into something else. Write a paragraph about what you would pick to turn into and why.

3. I wouldn't say I'm afraid of spiders, no matter what Flo thinks. But I definitely don't like them. Is there anything you're afraid of? Make me feel better, and write a paragraph about it.

# THE PROBLEMS WITH GOBLINS

Flo saw the creature kicking his feet and grunting as he squeezed his way outside. He landed on the fire escape with a *thud!*

Flo's mouth dropped open in shock. "What was that thing?" she asked.

Furry poked his head out the window. "A goblin! He went downstairs!" he cried.

"Good," Flo said. "Let him go! Don't we want the creepy goblin to stay outside? I sure don't want him in here!"

Furry shook his head. "You don't understand," he said, looking serious. "The problem with goblins is there's never just one."

# WANT MORE ADVENTURE?